The Silly Super Schnoodles

P Stevens

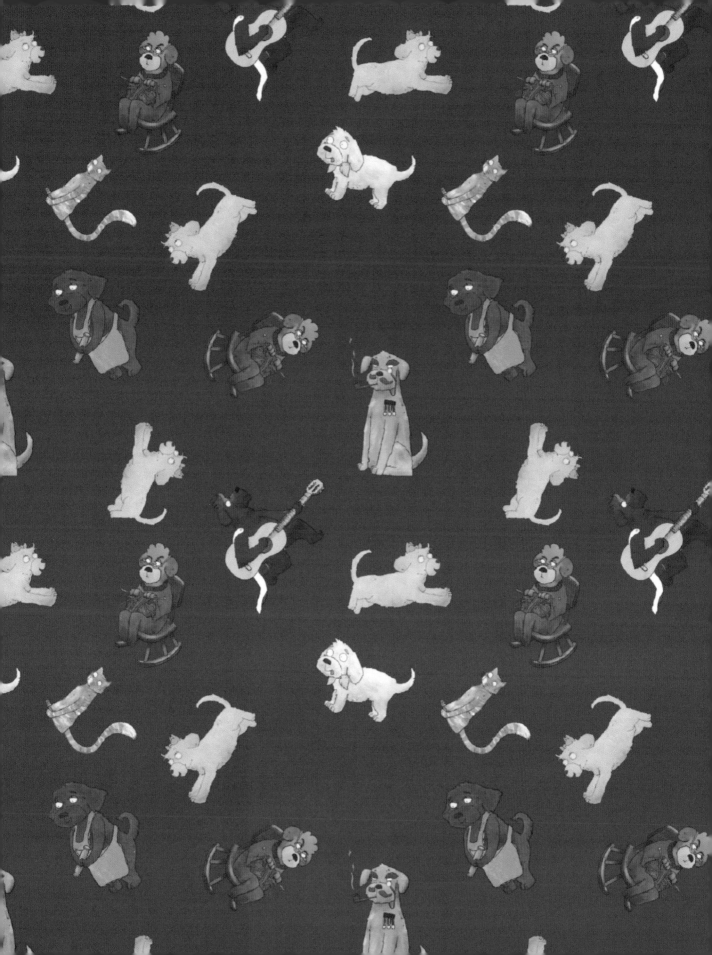

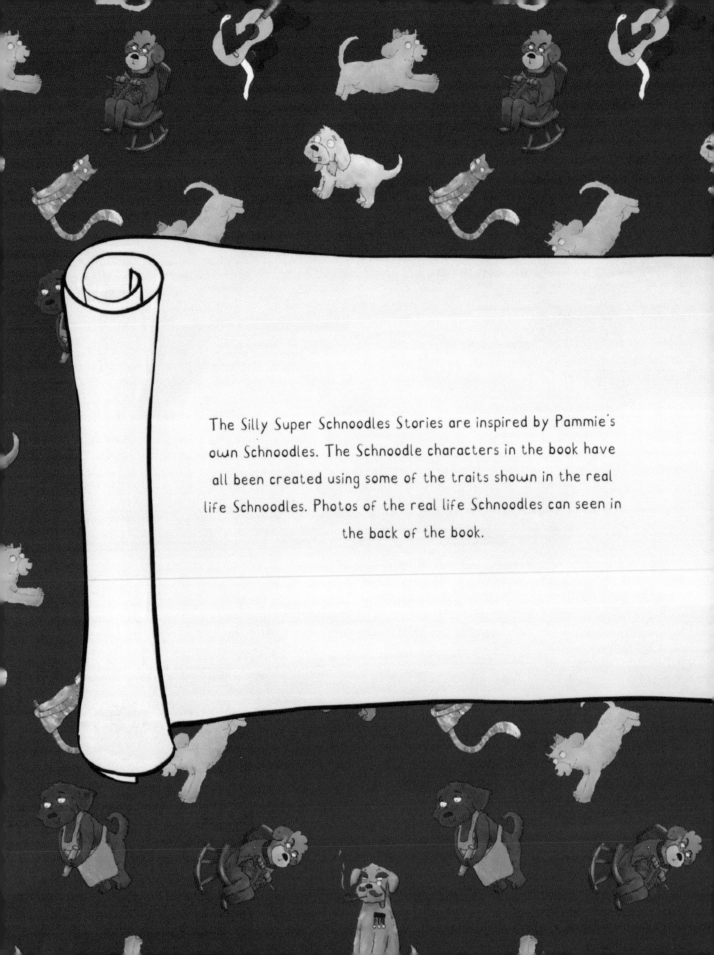

The Silly Super Schnoodles Stories are inspired by Pammie's own Schnoodles. The Schnoodle characters in the book have all been created using some of the traits shown in the real life Schnoodles. Photos of the real life Schnoodles can seen in the back of the book.

I would like to thank Judy & Haydn for their tireless
and tremendous help & support with ALL my Schnoodle
projects. Thanks to Judith and John for believing in me,
my Schnoodles and being a second home to Ralphie.
Happy Schnoodling Everyone!

Get to know the Silly

Frivolous Freda

scatty and excitable

Rocking Ralphie

Mumma V

sings out of tune and always
forgets the words

cooks magic cookies
for every occasion

Super Schnoodles

Friendly Freddie

a good Boy Scout

Cosmic the Cat

loves to tease Uncle Bundle

Nana Noodle

grumpy old lady,
knits all the time

Uncle Bundle

ex Army Officer,
enemy to all cats

The Silly Super Schnoodles were all watching the rain pour down outside. Suddenly, Uncle Bundle spotted Cosmic the Cat taking shelter under a bush.

He started barking orders. 'There's an imposter in our garden, quick march everybody, let's see him off!'

All the Silly Super Schnoodles, apart from Nana Noodle who stayed home to knit, scrambled to get their Silly Super Schnoodle wellie boots on and get out of the door,
The rain was ignored in the quest to follow Uncle Bundles Orders.

Once outside, the rain suddenly stopped.
The sun came out and a big, colourful
rainbow filled the sky.
Frivolous Freda, who had completely
forgotten about Cosmic the Cat, was
chasing the end of the rainbow with
excited glee. She leapt into the air but
Instead of landing on a pot of gold she
landed right in the middle of a big, deep,
splishy splashy puddle.
"Help! Help! Get me out", she began to
Shout! "My pink silly super schnoodle
wellies are stuck in the mud!"

Friendly Freddie was first on the scene and jumped
right in to try help get Frivolous Freda out.
Alas, it was too deep, and the water went over
the top of his green wellies too.

"Sorry Freda!" he called, as he hopped quickly back out of the splishy splashy puddle.

Mumma V was the next to wade in to try and rescue Frivolous Freda, but the water rushed in over the top of her red wellies too, she too had to turn round and come out of the splishy splashy puddle.

Rocking Ralphie was so busy singing, "rain, rain, go away" (dreadfully out of tune as normal!), he didn't notice the depth of the puddle until it was over the top of his blue wellies, so he reversed out of the Splishy, Splashy puddle.

Uncle Bundle had a plan!
He saw a rope hanging on a tree where
Cosmic the Cat had climbed up to get away
from him,
He asked Cosmic the Cat to throw it down
(which Cosmic did with a very smug look on
his feline face),
He waded out until the water was just under
his **black** wellies and threw the rope to
Frivolous Freda and barked orders to tie it
round her waste,
Once this was done, Uncle Bundle started to
heave and pull, but he couldn't pull Frivolous
Freda free,

He shouted, "Come on all you Silly Super Schnoodles, help pull Frivolous Freda out!"
So, all the Silly Super Schnoodles grabbed hold of the rope and began to heave and pull,

Suddenly Frivolous Freda flew over their heads
and landed on the grass next to the puddle,
She stood up in her in her Silly Super Schnoodle
Splishy, Splashy, Splooshy, Wooshy, Pink Wellies
and shouted, 'Yayyyyy, I'm out, I'm out of the big
Splishy, Splashy puddle'.

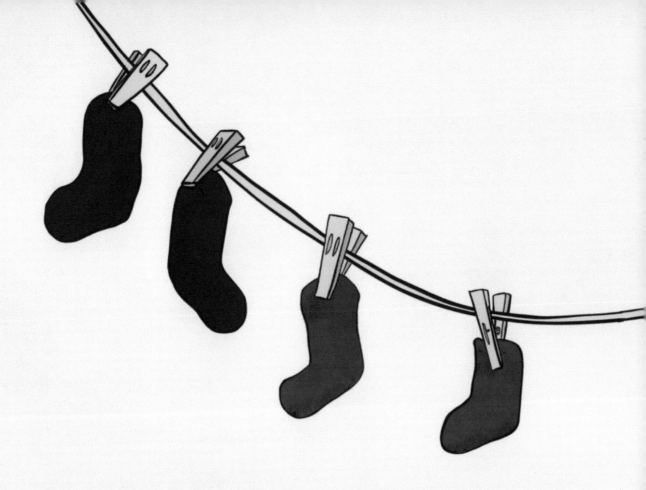

They all trudged home in their Silly Super Schnoodle
Splishy, Splashy, Splooshy, Wooshy Wellies.
When they got home, they discovered that Nana Noodle
had knitted them each a pair of lovely, long and warm

socks, (that matched the colour of their wellies!).
They all pulled off their Silly Super Schnoodle Splishy,
Splashy, Splooshy, Wooshy wellies and hung them up to
dry on the special wellie dryer.

They slipped on their lovely, long, warm socks and sat down in front of a lovely, warm log fire. They all had a cup of tea and some of Mumma V's magic, 'dry-your-paws-quickly' scones. Even Cosmic the Cat was allowed to join in!

How much do you remember about
The *Silly* Super Schnoodles
Splishy Splashy Saturday ?

1. Where was Cosmic the Cat sitting when Uncle Bundle spotted him from inside their house?

2. Which Silly Super Schnoodle stayed at home?

3. Which Silly Super Schnoodle went in to save Frivolous Freda first?

4. What colour were Mumma V's wellies?

5. Where did Frivolous Freda land when they finally managed to pull her out of the Splishy, Splashy puddle?

6. How many pairs of socks did Nana Noodle knit??

These are the real life Schnoodle characters that appear in the Silly Super Schnoodle Stories.

Uncle Bundle

Mumma V

Friendly Freddie

Frivolous Freda

Rocking Ralphie

Nana Noodle

" *They make ideal Pets because they are double non-shedding (both parent breeds are non-shedding), they have wonderful temperaments, they are very trainable, they are real characters (guaranteed to make you laugh everyday) and are the ideal size.*" Pammie Stevens

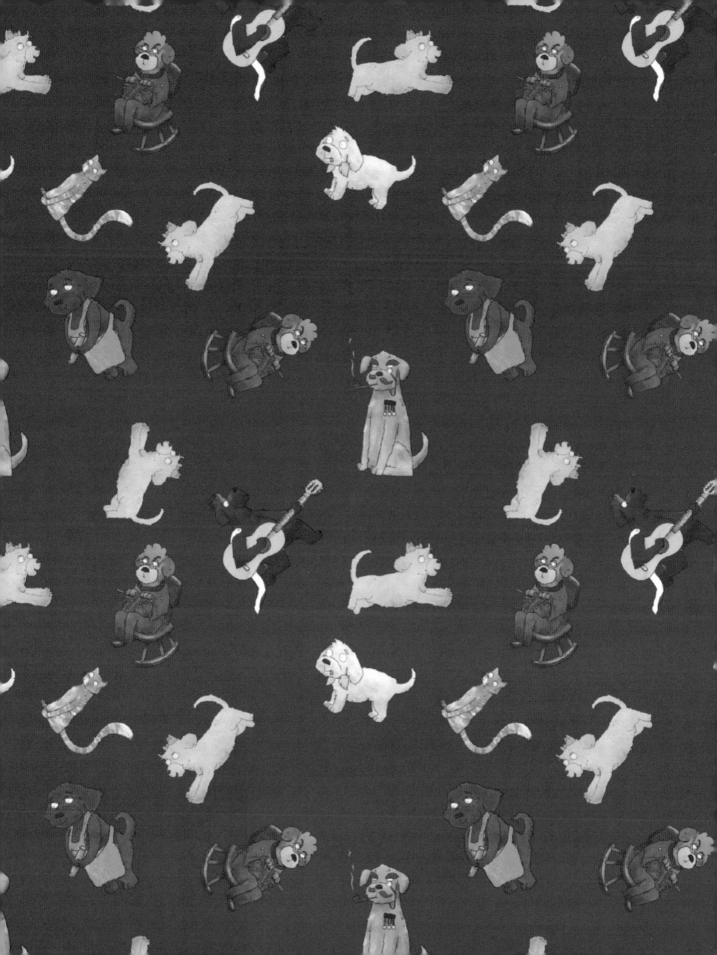

Printed in Poland
by Amazon Fulfillment
Poland Sp. z o.o., Wrocław

16960319R00018